A HORSE CALLED
Courage

ANNE SCHRAFF

PAGETURNERS®

ADVENTURE
  A Horse Called Courage
  Planet Doom
  The Terrible Orchid Sky
  Up Rattler Mountain
  Who Has Seen the Beast?

DETECTIVE
  The Case of the Bad Seed
  The Case of the Cursed Chalet
  The Case of the Dead Duck
  The Case of the Wanted Man
  The Case of the Watery Grave

MYSTERY
  The Hunter
  Once Upon a Crime
  Whatever Happened to Megan Marie?
  When Sleeping Dogs Awaken
  Where's Dudley?

SCIENCE FICTION
  Bugged!
  Escape from Earth
  Flashback
  Murray's Nightmare
  Under Siege

SPY
  A Deadly Game
  An Eye for an Eye
  I Spy, e-Spy
  Scavenger Hunt
  Tuesday Raven

SUSPENSE
  Boneyard
  The Cold, Cold Shoulder
  The Girl Who Had Everything
  Hamlet's Trap
  Roses Red as Blood

SADDLEBACK
EDUCATIONAL PUBLISHING
www.sdlback.com

ISBN: 978-1-68021-378-2
eBook: 978-1-63078-779-0

Printed in Malaysia

23 22 21 20 19   2 3 4 5 6

PAGETURNERS®|ADVENTURE

Chapter 1

Just think of it!" Sommer Oldham cried excitedly. "We can spend the summer working with horses. And get paid for it too!"

Vanessa Downey grabbed Sommer's hand. "You sure they'll hire us?" she asked. "Are you totally sure?"

"Yes." Sommer smiled. "My uncle owns the summer camp. He said he needs some teenage counselors to work with the little kids."

Standing nearby, Tami Nguyen smiled too. Sommer and Vanessa were not her best friends. But they were best friends with each other. Tami hadn't had a best friend in high school. She was shy. Making friends was hard.

Sometimes Tami tagged along with Vanessa and Sommer. But the two always talked to each other. They usually ignored her.

"How about you, Tami? Are you coming to work at Camp Colorado too?" Sommer asked. "I promised my uncle I could get two other girls besides myself."

"Oh yes," Tami said in surprise. She needed the money. But she didn't share the excitement and happiness of the other two girls. Tami feared being so far from home for the first time. Worse yet, she was terrified of horses!

The part of town where Tami lived was called Little Vietnam. Along with her parents, grandfather, and her three siblings, she felt safe and comfortable there. But next September Tami would be starting college. She needed to earn some money this summer. The Nguyen family had been struggling for a while. Tami was determined to pay for her own education.

♦ • ♦

"Grandfather," Tami said that night. "I think I can get a summer job at a children's camp. A girl I know from school is arranging it."

"Excellent," her grandfather said. Just after the fall of Saigon, he had escaped from Vietnam in a flimsy boat. Many of those with him had drowned. Pirates killed many more. But he had made it to the United States, along with his wife. With them they'd brought an orphaned boy who would become Tami's father.

"But I'm a little scared, Grandfather. Camp Colorado is up in the mountains. It's about a hundred miles from here," Tami said.

"We traveled over thousands of miles," Grandfather said with a smile. "You have not that far to go, Tami."

"I know," she said. "We'll have to ride the horses there. And I am afraid of horses."

"You must not let fear control you," Grandfather said. "You must say to yourself that you will be brave."

◆ ◆ ◆

A few days later, everyone applying for jobs at the camp was interviewed. Tami filled out the application. She tried to hide her fear when she spoke to the camp director. Like Sommer and Vanessa, Tami was hired immediately.

One week later all the camp employees gathered. They boarded a bus headed for Camp Colorado. Tami didn't know any of the passengers except Vanessa and Sommer. And of course those two girls shared a seat. They talked constantly to one another.

Tami sat alone, looking out the window. She didn't blame the girls for not paying attention to her. They had much more in common with each other than they did with her. Tami concentrated on feeling grateful.

This job would help her earn money for college.

The sun shined brightly. The bus rolled through traffic. Tami fought the desire to run away and hide. She had never been comfortable with strangers. And she was surrounded by teens she didn't know.

The bus began to climb the steep mountain road. "Isn't this exciting, Tami?" Vanessa said. "The only bummer is the cell reception sucks up here." It was the first time today that she had talked to Tami.

"Um, yes," she said, trying to sound enthusiastic. But in truth she was more frightened than excited. If she had been going camping with her family, she would have been truly happy.

Tami felt miserable. She knew she would miss dinner tonight. Her family would sit down to delicious *pho* and spring rolls. There would be yummy moon cakes for dessert. They were made from sweet rice and filled with bananas and raisins. The family would have a comfortable evening. Nothing unexpected would happen.

With her whole heart, Tami wished she could be there with them. The bus climbed the winding mountain road. She felt sadder as each mile took her farther from home.

Chapter 2

It was midmorning when the bus reached the camp. Camp Colorado was a beautiful place. There were many little log cabins. One very large cabin was for dining and recreation. A lake sparkled at the bottom of a hill. Sad as she was, Tami realized it really was a lovely setting.

Twenty young people filed out from the bus. The camp director met them with a clipboard.

"Hi, guys. I'm Dane Morgan," he said with a smile. He didn't look more than twenty, but he was confident and self-assured. Tami couldn't help but notice that he was handsome too. "First thing you need to do is to fill out these papers," he said. "Here's your chance to express your preferences. What kind of work do you want to do around here? We don't want to put any square pegs in round holes!"

Everybody laughed. All the girls giggled. They whispered to each other about how gorgeous Dane was. He had thick, curly hair and big brown eyes and dimples in his cheeks. Sommer nudged Vanessa. "Is he totally cool or what?" she said.

Tami looked over the list of available jobs: counselor, horseback riding, sports, crafts, kitchen help, maintenance. Sitting at one of the picnic tables, she quickly checked kitchen help. Ha! She would be happiest cutting up vegetables and running the dishwasher.

Vanessa and Sommer looked over at Tami. "We're putting horseback riding as first choice," Vanessa said. "That's the most fun. Be sure to write that down too, Tami."

Tami had never admitted her fear of

horses to the other girls. One day the three of them had gone riding in the park. Tami had been terrified the whole time. It didn't matter that her horse was as gentle as a big pussycat. Tami was ashamed of being such a timid person.

"Everybody will want that," Tami said. "So we may not all get it." Then she quickly folded her paper. It would be embarrassing if everyone saw that she had chosen to work in the kitchen. After all, the camp was about riding horses over the beautiful trails.

With any luck, Tami thought, she could spend her time slicing vegetables and making salads. That way she could avoid scary horses and strange people altogether.

"I put crafts as my second choice," Sommer said.

"Me too," Vanessa said. "What did you put for second choice, Tami?"

Tami had chosen maintenance. She would rather empty trash cans than face the horses. She didn't want to teach children how to make papier-mâché chickens either. "Crafts, yes," she lied.

"I wonder where Dane spends most of his time," Sommer said. "I'd sign up for anything to be where he was!"

"All right, you guys," Dane said. He had returned to collect the papers. "You can spend the next hour finding your bunks and getting settled. You'll get your assignments at lunchtime. The little kids don't start arriving until tomorrow. Enjoy the peace and quiet while it lasts. Or you can go riding or swimming this afternoon."

"Did you hear that?" Sommer whispered. "We can go riding!"

"Yeah," Vanessa said with a grin. She looked over at the big corral. Most of the horses were reddish-brown. There were a few black and mixed-color horses. One was silver-gray with a white mane.

"Do you see that silver beauty?" Sommer

cried. "Whoa! It's the color of smoke. Its mane is like spun silk. That's the one I'd like to ride!"

"That's Courage," Dane said. The girls hadn't seen him walk up behind them. "I'm afraid he's a very high-spirited animal. We don't usually let inexperienced riders ride him."

"Oh, come on, Dane! We're excellent riders," Sommer said.

Tami thought all the horses looked huge and dangerous. But the silver one did seem to be the fiercest of all.

"Do you ride?" Dane asked Tami. For a moment, she couldn't believe that the handsome guy was actually talking to her.

"Yes, but not very well," she said.

Dane smiled. "Well, that's okay. Being here will give you a good chance to become a better rider."

Vanessa and Sommer stared at Tami and Dane. They wondered why he had stopped to talk to her, of all people. There were several brunettes here at Camp Colorado. But Tami was the only Asian American girl. Maybe that's why Dane noticed her. She was exotic.

"Was your family from Vietnam?" Dane asked. He seemed genuinely interested in Tami.

"Yes," Tami said. "I was born here. My grandparents came to the United States with my dad."

Dane nodded. "My parents adopted my sisters from Korea five years ago. They had two boys—me and my brother—but they wanted girls too. Now I've got a six-year-old sister named Tiffany. The seven-year-old is named Brittany. They're so cute and a lot of fun."

Tami thought Dane was nice. It was odd for her to feel comfortable with a stranger. But she felt at home with him for some reason. Maybe it was because he had such a friendly way about him.

When Dane walked away, Vanessa and Sommer rushed over to Tami. Sommer had an angry look in her eyes. "What's the deal? Do you know him from somewhere?" she demanded.

"No. I never saw him before today," Tami said. "But he seems very nice."

"Wow, you're a really a big flirt!" Vanessa said in a rude voice. "Aren't you, Tami? It was gross. I couldn't believe how you were throwing yourself at him!"

Chapter 3

Tami was shocked and hurt. "I was not flirting," she said defensively. "I was surprised when he came to talk to me." She was upset that her friends would turn against her for no good reason. She could tell they liked Dane. They must be jealous that he was talking to her and not to them. But that was not her fault. How could they blame her?

The jobs were passed out at lunchtime. Tami got kitchen duty. The other girls got riding.

"What did you get?" Sommer called out to Vanessa. "I got helping the kids with riding class!"

"Me too," Vanessa said happily. "I bet

Dane is really into horses too. We'll see a lot of him."

The girls turned to Tami then. "Did you get riding too?" Sommer asked.

"No. I'll be helping in the kitchen," Tami said.

Sommer and Vanessa exchanged looks. How could Tami have ended up with such a bad assignment? But they were secretly glad. If Dane liked her, he wouldn't be seeing much of her in the kitchen!

After lunch Dane was saddling a horse. The teen counselors clustered around him. Sommer and Vanessa hurried to join in.

Dane smiled at the eager faces. "Let's go for a short ride," he said. "I'd like to see how well each of you can ride before the kids arrive. Even you guys who aren't signed up to teach riding classes should learn how to handle a horse. It's part of your job at Camp Colorado."

Tami tried to slip away. But Dane looked

at her. He said, "I'd like everybody in on this."

Tami trembled at the thought of riding. She was only five three. She weighed ninety-six pounds. When she rode a horse, she felt out of control and nervous. "I … I'm kind of afraid of horses," Tami finally admitted.

Sommer giggled behind her hand. She could imagine what a turn-off that would be to Dane. "You're kidding me, Tami," Sommer said loudly enough for Dane to hear. "You're afraid of a mellow horse at a kids' camp?"

Tami blushed with embarrassment. "Yes. It's the truth," she said. "They are such big animals. I just don't feel safe on a horse."

Dane smiled at a dark-haired girl. She rode out of the corral with perfect form. "Nice handling!" he shouted. "Nice posture, Bella."

Sommer was eager to show Dane her own riding skills. She also thought it would be funny if Dane could see how awkward Tami was on a horse. Sommer remembered the day they had all gone riding in the park. Tami's back wasn't straight. She had hunched over in an awkward, funny way.

The truth was that Sommer was jealous. Seeing Dane smiling so warmly at Tami made her angry. Now she smirked. What would Dane think of Tami if he saw how stupid she looked in the saddle? Sommer grabbed Tami's hand. "Come on, Tami. Let's go," she said. "You can ride okay. It'll be fun."

Vanessa joined in the effort to force Tami to ride. Both of them wanted to make her look silly.

"No … please … I'm afraid," Tami groaned. She tried to pull away.

Tami was confused by her friends' insistence that she ride. She thought they must be doing this for her own good. They only wanted her to have some fun. The girls simply couldn't understand anyone who didn't like horseback riding. At that point it never dawned on Tami that her friends were trying to humiliate her in front of Dane.

"Tami wants to ride that black horse," Sommer said to Dane.

Dane smiled and brought the horse over.

"Come on, Tami. I'll show you how to mount," Dane said. He helped her into the saddle.

She was shaking all over, hoping he didn't notice.

"Just hold the reins like this," Dane said. "Grasp the horse's mane."

Tami felt like she might fall off the saddle at any moment. She heard several of the other girls giggling at her obvious discomfort.

Now humiliation was added to her fear. She could imagine the horse throwing her to the ground. Then it would walk passively away. Her humiliation would be complete.

Sommer and Vanessa mounted their horses smoothly. They made it a point to ride past where Dane stood.

"Nice hold on the reins," Dane told Sommer.

"Good, good," he said to Vanessa. "You're using your legs just right to control the horse. Good knee pressure on the turns!"

Then Dane's voice suddenly rose in alarm. "Tami, no, no! You're not balancing right. You're digging both knees into the horse. He doesn't know what to do. You're telling him to go left and right at the same time."

Tami was terrified. The black horse was starting to trot off. She couldn't control him. How could she stop him? When she yanked on the reins, the horse snorted in rage.

Sommer and Vanessa exchanged amused looks. Tami was making such a fool of herself! Now Dane could see what a silly girl she was.

Dane ran after Tami's horse. He tried to catch up before there was an accident.

"She's making a real mess of it," Sommer said, snickering.

"Dane is so disgusted. Look at how angry he looks," Vanessa said.

Dane finally caught the reins of the horse and stopped him. He could see tears running down Tami's cheeks.

"I'm sorry!" she gasped. "I'm so sorry!"

Chapter 4

That's okay," Dane said kindly. "Nobody is born a good rider. It takes a lot of practice. This isn't the horse for you anyway, Tami. He's not too patient with inexperienced riders. Blackjack wasn't the best horse to choose. I don't know why you chose him."

He didn't know she hadn't chosen the black horse. Sommer had.

Dane helped her down from the saddle. He took a firm hold of her arm. "There we go," he said with a warm smile. "I'll give you your next riding lesson soon. Marshmallow is the horse for you. She's a sweetheart. A beginner could do everything wrong and still have a good ride."

Sommer's joy at Tami's wretched ride

quickly turned to anger and frustration. Dane was not disgusted by Tami's lack of skill. He was being extra nice and helpful to her. Her stupidity was endearing to him! Kind and reassuring, Dane patted her on the back. He led her to a bench. Tami sat while he went to get some water.

Dane didn't go out on the trail ride. He stayed behind to comfort Tami.

"Oh, she's clever!" Sommer said bitterly. "Look! She's got Dane wrapped around her little finger. Ugh! The little witch."

"You think she acted scared on purpose?" Vanessa asked. "To get Dane to pity her?"

"Yeah, I do," Sommer said. "Tami's really sneaky. She pretended to be scared just so Dane would rescue her."

The rest of the counselors rode off toward the hills. Tami sat and sipped her water. "I am so ashamed to be afraid of horses," she said to Dane. "I'm sure they are nice animals. I think almost everybody likes them."

Dane laughed. "It's okay. We're all afraid of something or other. Some people are afraid of dogs," he said.

"I rode with the other girls last year. We went all through the park on the bridle path. But I never liked it," Tami said. "I thought they wouldn't like me if I didn't pretend to love horseback riding too. It's not easy for me to make friends. I didn't want to lose the few I had."

"Well, a lot of people do get hurt riding horses. It's like everything else, Tami. You need to know what you're doing. Once you learn to ride well, it's a pretty safe sport," he said. "Just relax. Stay away from the horses for a while. Then you can take another shot at it. I'll give you some lessons on Marshmallow. Who knows? You might end up enjoying it."

Tami smiled gratefully at him.

Dane didn't make fun of her. He didn't make her feel ashamed for being afraid.

Tami liked him very much. Back in high school, Tami hadn't dated any boys. Sometimes she went out with a group of boys and girls. But never had she gone on a date with a boy. There hadn't been any boys she liked well enough to date. Her parents thought that was just fine. They said she was too young for dating anyway.

But Dane was very different. Tami thought maybe he was someone she would enjoy spending time with.

In the evening the camp staff gathered around tables in the recreation cabin. The children would be arriving tomorrow. Dane gave instructions. Everyone was given tips on how to deal with anxious parents and homesick kids. He talked about bullies, loners, and troublemakers.

Tami sat alone at a table. Then Sommer joined her. Sommer burned with curiosity. She had to know what had happened between Tami and Dane that afternoon. The other counselors had been out riding.

"Hi, Tami," Sommer said. "Did you and Dane get everything squared away about horseback riding?"

"Yes. I told him how afraid I was of horses. He was super nice and sweet," Tami said. "He was very chill about it."

"Yeah," Sommer said. "He feels sorry for you. You made a fool of yourself almost falling off the horse. Here's a warning, Tami. Don't pester Dane, okay? I mean, Vanessa and I brought you along with us. We don't want you to make us look bad. Dane is a really busy guy. He hasn't got time for somebody who's needy. He has to think about the little kids coming tomorrow. He can't hold the hand of some crybaby counselor, you know?"

Tami was shocked by the harshness of Sommer's words. A terrible thought came to her. Had Dane complained to Sommer about her? Had he said that she was causing him trouble? He seemed so nice and thoughtful. Could he have gone behind her back to ridicule her? "Sommer," Tami said. "Did Dane say he was upset with me?"

Sommer shrugged. "Oh, he's too nice to come right out and say that. But I overheard him talking to some of the other guys. He said some of the counselors they've hired are more babyish than the little kids." Sommer carefully built her lie to sound believable. "He said something about one stupid girl who had messed up with a horse. He said he shuddered to think of such a fool working with little kids."

Tami felt like somebody had slapped her across the face. Dane had seemed so kind and understanding! But it was all a lie. He was laughing at her. Making fun of her to his friends. Now she made up her mind to avoid him at all costs.

Tami was assigned to Cabin 6. There

was room for a counselor and four children. Each cabin was like that.

It was early on the morning of the second day. Tami met her four charges. The girls ranged in age from eight to ten. Tami had two little sisters. She was sure she could get along with these lively little campers.

Pearl was an athletic eight-year-old. She was eager to join in the activities. Leah, a tall, artistic nine-year-old, was most interested in the craft classes. Liz was a chubby, sweet-natured ten-year-old. She wanted to swim all day. Aneal, at age nine, was moody. She seemed sure that everybody hated her. Aneal would need the most attention, Tami thought.

"I heard there are rattlesnakes here. And coyotes in the hills," Pearl said. "I sure hope we get to see some of them. Will we, Tami?"

"I'm sure we'll see animals on our hikes," Tami said with a smile.

Just then, there was a knock on the cabin door. Tami was surprised to see Dane standing there. Now it was hard for her to look into those warm brown eyes. She had trusted him too quickly. Everything was different now. She knew what he had said behind her back.

Chapter 5

"May I talk to you outside for a minute, Tami?" Dane asked.

"Of course," she said. Without looking at him, she stepped outside. Then she closed the door behind her. Her heart ached. Sommer's words the day before had been so cruel.

"I want to tell you about Aneal, one of your girls," Dane said. "She's an unhappy kid who can't make friends easily. I'm afraid she's been caught in the middle of a bitter custody fight between her parents. They've been saying poisonous words about each other. Each parent is trying to turn Aneal against the other. She's angry at the world, I'm afraid. So please give her a little extra attention, Tami. She needs it," Dane said.

"Of course, I will," Tami said, staring at the ground. She could not bear to look directly at him.

Dane smiled warmly. "I sense that you have the right skills to reach her. You have simpatico," he said.

Tami finally looked at him. *Simpatico*? What did that word mean? She had not heard it before. Sommer said Dane had talked about a stupid girl who couldn't handle a horse. Maybe simpatico was another word for stupid. "What does *simpatico* mean?" she asked nervously.

"It's a Spanish word that means understanding," Dane said. "My mom is from Colombia."

"Oh," Tami said. Her lips trembled with the mix of emotions she felt. "I want to apologize again for the trouble I had riding that horse. I know it annoyed you very much. I want you to know how very sorry I am."

"Annoyed me?" he asked in surprise. "Not at all. I—"

Tami cut in before he could go on. "A friend told me what you said. You haven't got time for stupid girls who almost fall off their horses. She told me you said you can't trust them with the children when they do things like that," she said nervously.

Dane looked shocked. "I never said anything like that, Tami! Whoever told you that I did is lying for some reason. I never even thought anything like that. Your friend is a liar. I'm sorry to be so blunt. But that's the way it is."

Tami hurried back inside the cabin. Now she was totally confused. Would Sommer make up such a thing? Why? She didn't have to think long before coming up with a reason. Sommer must be jealous of her!

Back in high school, Sommer had wanted the attention of every good-looking guy. She was probably the prettiest girl in the senior class. And she knew it. Sommer thought she was entitled to first choice. Now she was angry with Tami for distracting Dane.

In the morning, everybody gathered outside for a big breakfast. Pancakes. Sausages. Eggs. For an hour or so, Tami was busy frying sausages and eggs and flipping pancakes. When she was finally done, she found a table over on the side. She sat down to eat her breakfast. She deliberately chose a place far from Vanessa and Sommer. Two campers from her cabin, Pearl and Leah, sat down at her table.

"You're nice," Pearl said. "I'm glad you're our camp counselor, Tami. You let us stay up a little after dark."

"Yeah," Leah agreed. "And thanks for telling us that great Vietnamese ghost story.

That was so cool. You're extra special, Tami."

"She sure is," said a male voice.

Tami hadn't seen Dane walk up. Now he was standing right beside her. His plate was loaded with food. "May I join you?"

He was wearing a big white apron. There was a pink cartoon pig on the front. Tami thought he looked dreamy.

"Sure," Tami said, smiling at him. Last night he had denied saying those ugly things. And she had believed him.

They sat eating for a while. Then Dane wandered off to make some more pancakes. The moment he was gone, Pearl and Leah sang, *"Tami has a boyfriend! Tami has a boyfriend!"*

Then Pearl giggled. Both little girls said they thought Dane was as hot as a movie star. The two then went off to play a game of soccer.

Sommer came walking toward Tami's

table. On the way, she stopped at the griddle where Dane was cooking. Tami could hear her singsong voice.

"Wow, Dane! Looking good this morning. They shouldn't let a guy as cute as you run loose among all these little girls. Pretty soon they'll start squealing and screaming like rock star fans," Sommer said.

Tami could tell Dane was embarrassed and annoyed. Sommer was too bold sometimes. One time she had flirted with boys at school so much that she was called into the principal's office for being disruptive. Another time she tweeted pictures of herself in a skimpy bathing suit. She got in trouble for that too. Sommer simply couldn't understand why any guy would not fall crazy in love with her.

"The pancakes are really good, aren't they?" Dane said. He ignored Sommer's bait. "And the sausage too. Are you on the kitchen staff? If so, you've done a great job."

"Me?" Sommer laughed. "I don't get near any kitchen, thank you very much. You remember me, don't you? I'm the girl you complimented for riding so well that first day."

"Sorry," Dane said. "Until I get to know you, you girls all look alike to me. But keep up the good work with your riding. The little kids are all eager to get on a horse. We need good riders to help them."

Sommer did a slow burn. She hated being snubbed. It was unthinkable!

Tami remembered their junior year. A beautiful French exchange student had shown up at school. The boys fell instantly in love. Sommer was kicked to the curb. And she was furious about it. She had called the poor girl all the terrible names she could think of behind her back.

Then someone had poured heavy-duty glue into the French girl's purse. It had cemented her lipstick, mirror, and even ID card together. Then she had reached into her purse. The sticky glue bonded her two fingers to the mess. She had to go to the school nurse to get the stuff off. The poor girl had been hysterical.

Nobody could ever prove who had committed the ugly prank. But Tami had always believed it was Sommer.

Chapter 6

Tami had some free time. Her charges had all vanished to their classes. She took a walk around the camp. She even ventured near the corrals.

Tami looked at all the horses, finally spotting Marshmallow. This was the gentle horse Dane thought she could ride. She was a dappled horse with white spots. The horse was just as big as the others. But her beautiful brown eyes looked peaceful somehow.

Tami climbed the corral fence. She gingerly reached out her hand to pat Marshmallow on the nose. It was as soft as the smoothest velvet. Marshmallow nickered softly. But then she broke into a trot. Tami jumped back, startled.

"You're such a chicken," snapped a voice behind Tami. "That horse just barely moved. And you almost jumped out of your skin!"

"Sommer," Tami said. "Why are you being so mean to me? I did nothing to hurt you. You even lied about what Dane said about me. He never said those mean things."

Sommer's eyes narrowed. The beauty of her face disappeared. Jealousy made her eyes beady and her skin red. She looked downright ugly now. "It's just so disgusting how you're chasing Dane. Everybody sees what you're doing! You wear your jeans so tight. They look like they're painted on. We've watched you wriggle around in front of him every chance you get," Sommer said.

"My jeans are no different from yours or anyone else's," Tami said. "I've never flirted with Dane. Give me a break, Sommer. I don't know why you are acting like this."

"Well," Sommer said with a toss of her hair. "Your boyfriend said to tell you to meet him in the barn. I guess he wants to teach you how to sit on a horse. You'd better hurry over there before he gets impatient."

"If he wants to see me, it must be about the girls in my cabin. It must be important," Tami said. She turned and walked toward the barn. Maybe Dane wanted to tell her more about Aneal. The poor little girl did seem very sad. Tami wanted to help her if she could.

Reaching the barn, Tami pushed the door open. "Dane?" she called out.

It was so dark inside. Tami tried to adjust her eyes. She could make out some stacked bales of hay over in the corner. There was no sign of Dane.

"Dane?" Tami called out again.

Suddenly the narrow barn door filled up with the shape of a horse. Someone had shooed it into the barn. The door slammed shut. Now Tami was trapped in the barn with the horse! Then Tami heard the click of a padlock on the outside of the door.

"No!" Tami screamed. She backed away from the nervous, snorting horse. It was the smoke-colored horse. The horse called Courage. Dane had said it was too spirited for an inexperienced rider.

Courage restlessly pawed the sawdust floor. He whinnied excitedly. Tami was terrified of being kicked or trampled by the frightened horse. She tried to climb to safety on the bales of hay. But she couldn't get a footing.

"Help!" Tami screamed. Now Courage was pitching and bucking like a wild bronco. The horse's fear of the close quarters and the darkness grew.

Tami didn't see who had shooed Courage into the barn. But she had a good idea who it was. Sommer must have deliberately lied to her about Dane calling her to the barn!

She knew how scared Tami was of horses. Sommer had apparently trapped her there with the most dangerous horse in the stable.

"Help!" Tami screamed again. She backed along the walls of the barn, trying to evade the heavy, thrashing hooves. "Help! Somebody help!" she cried. She had never been so frightened in all her life. But as loudly as she screamed, her cries for help were lost. The camp was noisy with happy kids playing in the swimming pool and on the volleyball courts.

Then Courage suddenly kicked violently at the barn wall. A shaft of light came pouring in. Tami rushed over and pushed aside that board and the one next to it. In a moment she was out. She moved fast across the meadow. Tami ran toward the first adult she saw. A horse had been locked in the barn, she said. And it needed to be freed.

Vanessa and Sommer were in the pool, splashing with the children. Tami walked to the edge of the pool and just stood there, staring. Finally Sommer turned and caught her eye. Tami gave her a withering look. Then she quickly walked away.

She wasn't sure what would happen if she told the camp director what Sommer had done. After all, Sommer's uncle owned the camp. Would Sommer be packing her bags before the end of the day? Tami doubted it. Besides, she didn't want to ruin Sommer's job. She needed money for college too.

Tami decided that from now on she would stay completely away from Sommer and Vanessa. After all, high school was over. They were all going to different colleges in the fall. It made her sad that she would no longer be friends with the two girls she had known all through high school. But there was no other way now. What else could she do?

Chapter 7

Tami walked toward her cabin. She saw Aneal sitting by herself on a rough log bench.

"Hi, Aneal," Tami said softly. "Why aren't you swimming? The other girls are having lots of fun in the pool."

"I don't like to swim," Aneal said.

"Why don't you join the softball game?" Tami asked.

"I don't want to," Aneal said. "I don't like people. I'd rather sit here by myself and feed the squirrels."

"Don't you like any people?" Tami asked with a small smile.

"Nope," the little girl said firmly.

"How come?" Tami asked.

"I'm afraid of them," Aneal said. She twirled one of her dark pigtails. Then she wrapped it around her finger. "Just when you get to like them, they run off and leave you alone."

"Did somebody important run away from you, Aneal?" Tami asked softly.

"Uh-huh," the little girl said. "My dad did. Then Mom got a boyfriend. He was pretty nice. He took me riding on his motorcycle. After a while, though, he ran away too. Then my mom got another boyfriend. They ran off together and left me with my dad. A couple of months later Mom came back. And now she wants me back," Aneal said. "But Dad says no. The two of them are fighting all the time. I don't know where I'm going to go or anything. So I'm scared to get mixed up with people."

"I'm scared too," Tami said.

"You are?" Aneal asked in surprise. "Did people run off on you too?"

"No. I'm a little scared of being with people. Because I'm shy. I'm always thinking that people won't like me. Or that I'll make a fool of myself. And I'm scared of horses too," Tami admitted.

"Scared of horses?" Aneal almost laughed. "Horses are the best! How could anybody be afraid of horses? I like horses better than people."

"I bet you're a good rider," Tami said with an encouraging smile.

"Oh, I'm okay, I guess. I do love horses, though. I love horses more than anything in the whole world," Aneal said in a serious voice.

"But they're so big. Aren't you afraid of being thrown off?" Tami asked. "It's so far down from the saddle to the ground. And what if the horse kicks you?"

Aneal laughed out loud. "You're kidding me! Is that what scares you? Really? Oh, that's the funniest thing I ever heard."

Tami was glad she had made Aneal laugh. At least she was having some success as a counselor.

"Maybe someday I won't be afraid of horses," Tami said. "Dane said there's a real nice horse named Marshmallow. Maybe I'll try to ride her. Maybe then, little by little, I won't be afraid of horses anymore. And maybe someday you won't be afraid of people. Not all people run away, you know."

"Maybe," Aneal said. After a moment's silence she looked up. "I like talking to you, Tami. I've been to camp before. I've talked to lots of doctors and stuff. You know, like psy-psy—"

"Psychologists?" Tami filled in.

"Yeah, them. But I like talking to you better. Those people talk funny. They think

I'm just a dumb little kid who doesn't know what's good for me and stuff," Aneal said.

♦ ♦ ♦

Later, Tami walked past the corrals. She noticed that Courage was in a special enclosure. He had a bandage on his leg. Maybe he had hurt himself when he kicked the board out of the barn wall.

Tami caught up to the veterinarian. He was checking over all the horses. "Is Courage all right?" she asked him. "He's not badly hurt or anything, is he?"

"He'll be fine. Just got scratched up a little bit. We're going to rest him for a while," the man said.

Aneal joined Tami at the corral fence. "Courage is my favorite horse," she said. "Last year when I came here, I got to ride him all the way up to Eagle Point. Everybody said he was real spirited. But the two of us got along fine. I want to ride him tomorrow when the first group goes out."

"I don't think Courage will be riding tomorrow," Tami said. "Some mean person locked him in the old hay barn today. He got so upset that he kicked a hole in the wall. He hurt his leg a little bit."

♦ • ♦

Just as Tami had thought, in the morning all the horses were saddled up, but not Courage. Most of the children went on the morning ride. A few stayed behind to swim or work on crafts they had started. Only a skeleton crew was there to keep an eye on the few campers who were left.

Tami didn't go on the ride. She didn't want to take part in any activity that Vanessa and Sommer were involved in. Dane had said she should go. Marshmallow wouldn't hurt her. But at the last minute she had lost her nerve. She just couldn't make herself climb up onto one of those big horses.

When Dane saddled up for the ride, Tami

noticed that Sommer was grinning from ear to ear. Here was her chance to have a whole day in the outdoors with him. Surely that would wake him up to how beautiful and desirable she was. Without pesky Tami to distract him, Dane was bound to give in to Sommer's charms. That was her belief and hope.

The large group of riders had saddled up. They moved slowly toward the trail. Aneal changed her mind about going. "If Courage can't go, then I won't go either," she'd said.

"Courage wouldn't mind if you went on another horse and had some fun," Tami said. She thought it would be a shame for the little girl to miss out on the day's adventure. Aneal loved riding so much.

"No," Aneal said. "Anyway, I think my dad is coming to pick me up today. Grandma said that he and his new girlfriend might come get me."

"Would you like that, Aneal?" Tami asked the little girl.

"Yeah. My dad lives over there in Cottonwood," Aneal said, pointing west toward the foothills. "It's not far. Daddy has horses too. Maybe he can buy Courage for me. Then we can keep him in Cottonwood so I can ride him when I visit."

Tami felt sorry for Aneal. She doubted that the little girl's father was coming for her. It was probably just wishful thinking. Maybe he didn't even live in Cottonwood anymore.

"I guess I'll go swimming," Aneal said, walking toward the pool. Three or four children were already splashing around. A lifeguard kept a watchful eye on them.

Tami went to the kitchen. She had to help the cooks cut up vegetables and meat for tonight's big barbecue. When the horseback riders returned in the early evening, they would have shish kebab for dinner. The women in the kitchen were not counselors like Tami. They were regular employees.

Today only six employees remained at the camp. There were the cooks. Two older men, the lifeguard, and crafts teacher were also on duty.

After Tami was finished helping in the kitchen, she went to check on Aneal. She looked for her in the pool. But she couldn't see her among the bobbing heads. She wasn't there.

Tami was alarmed. "Where is Aneal?" she asked the lifeguard.

"She said she was feeling sick," the man said. "She went back to her cabin to rest."

Tami hurried to the cabin. "Aneal," she called out as she opened the door. "Are you okay?"

But no one was there to answer her. The cabin was empty.

A note with a neatly printed message was resting on Aneal's pillow.

Dear Tami,

I'm going to Dad's house. I'm hiking to Cottonwood.

Love ya,
Aneal

Chapter 8

Aneal's note made Tami recoil in shock. She rushed outside and ran to the pool. "Mr. Irwin," she said to the lifeguard. "Aneal is hiking down to Cottonwood by herself! She left a note!"

"Cottonwood?" Mr. Irwin cried. "That's sixty miles west of here. It's over some rugged canyons and ravines. No way a little kid is going to make it that far. In fact, it's dangerous for a kid to be out there at all. There's a horse trail leading over there, but …"

Tami thought quickly. "Do you ride, Mr. Irwin?" she asked.

"No, I don't. I never rode a horse in my life," the lifeguard said.

"Does the craft teacher ride?" Tami asked hopefully.

"Nope. She's sixty-nine years old. And she's got arthritis. Look, young lady, you are a camp counselor. I'm sure you could jump onto a horse and catch up to the little girl in no time," Mr. Irwin said.

Tami's heart sank. She had never ridden a horse farther than half a mile. And that was on a bridle path in the park! Worse still, the only horse left in the corral was a high-spirited horse with a sore leg. The big silver horse would probably refuse to let her ride him, even if she tried.

"I wonder … if I followed the trail on foot, could I catch up to Aneal?" Tami asked.

The lifeguard shrugged. "Guess you could try. But if that little kid started off a while ago, she could've gone pretty far. She could be in trouble already, tumbling into a ravine or meeting up with a rattlesnake.

I'll call the sheriff right now. They'll send a search team. But if I were you, I'd jump onto that silver horse now and take off after the girl. The sheriff will come as soon as he can. But you'd be able to get to her first. Time might be important."

Mr. Irwin helped saddle Courage. Then he helped her astride. "Follow the trail," he advised. "And yell out her name real loud. Good luck to you."

Tami's heart was pounding wildly. She tried to remember all the horseback riding tips she had ever heard. *Keep your back straight. Keep your weight slightly forward. If you want to turn left, shift your weight to the left. To go right, press your right knee.*

All the advice was a jumble in her brain. Courage headed for the trail. Tami leaned forward. She whispered desperately, "Please, Courage, find her! Please!"

Courage moved slowly down the trail

at first. But then he broke into a trot. Swallowing her panic, Tami hung on, shouting Aneal's name.

"Aneal! Aneal!" she yelled.

But the horse was going too fast! How could she get him to slow down? Now Courage was actually galloping down the dusty trail. His hooves kicked up clods of dirt. Tami was afraid she would fly off at any moment. She imagined cracking her head on one of the boulders that lined the trail.

"Slow down!" Tami shouted. "Oh, Courage, please slow down!" But the big silver horse galloped on.

Tami racked her brain in an effort to remember the riding instructions. *Shift your weight slightly backward. Squeeze with your legs. Use the reins to slightly increase pressure on the horse's mouth.*

Tami's face broke out in a cold sweat as the rocky landscape flew past.

Chapter 9

Tami could hardly believe it! Courage had slowed to a trot.

"It worked! It worked!" she whispered gratefully. She was shaking so hard that the reins almost fell from her hands. Then she recovered her voice. She started shouting Aneal's name once again.

"Aneal! Where are you?" Tami yelled loudly.

"Over here," a child's voice called out. Aneal was sitting atop a large, smooth boulder. "I got tired," she said. "So I stopped to take a little rest."

The girl started to climb down from the giant rock. Tami heard a strange buzzing sound. It came from the brush at the foot of the boulder. She knew rattlesnakes lived in the canyons. Could that actually be a rattlesnake in the tall weeds just below Aneal's dangling feet?

"Don't move!" Tami shouted. "Don't move an inch! I'm coming, Aneal."

But first she had to get off the big horse. She didn't know how. Tami held the reins and gingerly swung her leg over the horse. Then she clumsily dropped to the ground, nearly falling on her face. The startled horse almost reared up. But Tami hung on to the reins. She led him to a small tree, tying the reins firmly.

Then Tami began walking slowly toward the boulder where Aneal sat waiting. "Don't move," she said again. She could see it now. There was a huge rattlesnake, with its telltale diamond pattern and large rattle. The weeds moved as the snake crawled from under the boulder. Its enormous body seemed to lumber along like a miniature freight train with many cars. "Don't move, Aneal," Tami repeated in a deliberately calm voice.

"Why not?" Aneal asked.

"There's a rattlesnake at the bottom of the boulder. I don't want you to upset him," Tami explained.

"A real rattlesnake?" Aneal said with more curiosity than fear. "Wow! Show me. Where is it?"

"Aneal, don't move! Snakes strike at moving objects," Tami said. She had learned that fact during counselor orientation.

The rattlesnake had finally moved off into the grass. Tami hurried to Aneal. Taking her hand, she helped the little girl down from the boulder. "I want you to come back to camp now."

"Back to camp? But what about going to Cottonwood?" Aneal asked.

"Your father can find you at camp,"

Tami said. "We're having a wonderful shish-kebab barbecue tonight. I want you to sit at my table. Okay?"

"I guess so," Aneal said.

With a mighty heave, Tami boosted Aneal up onto Courage's back. Then she climbed on herself. She felt almost as nervous as before.

"How come you're shaking, Tami?" Aneal asked.

"I told you I was scared of horses," Tami said.

"Don't be scared," Aneal said. "I'll help you tell Courage what to do."

"Thanks, Aneal," Tami said.

"Tami, you're scared of horses. How come you rode Courage and came after me?" Aneal asked.

"Because I was worried about you, Aneal," Tami said sternly. "I was afraid you'd slip and fall into a canyon. Or that a snake would bite you. You shouldn't have come out here by yourself. Somebody had to come get you. And there was nobody else but me. I'm not brave, but I had to do it."

"Well, I think you're brave, Tami. Grandma told me that when you do something you're really scared of, then you're brave. One time I was scared to go to the dentist. But I went anyway. My grandma said that proved I was brave. She says that only scared people who go ahead in spite of their fear can be called brave," Aneal said.

Tami smiled. She reached down and patted Courage's silky mane. "Courage is brave too, isn't he? After all, his leg hurt. And he must have known that a foolish girl was riding him. But he came through, didn't he?"

By the time the two rode into camp, the sheriff had arrived. A search party was being organized. A big cheer went up when everyone saw Aneal riding with Tami.

◆ ◆ ◆

At the shish-kebab barbecue that evening, Tami's rescue of Aneal was the main topic of conversation. Dane sat beside her. "You sure overcame your fear of horses today, Tami. When push came to shove, you came through with flying colors."

Tami smiled. "I guess I was more worried about Aneal than I was about riding. But I still don't feel comfortable on top of a horse," she said, laughing.

She walked to her cabin that night. And it dawned on her that she didn't have a girlfriend to talk to about her day. At the barbecue, she had glanced around at the faces of the other counselors. But everybody seemed to have made friends already. Tami would have felt funny pushing her way into one of the cozy little circles that were already formed.

"But," Tami said out loud. "I have to start somewhere. When I get to college, everybody I meet will be a stranger. I must learn how to reach out. I don't want to be shy for my entire life."

Chapter 10

Outside her cabin, Tami noticed a girl with long blonde hair. She looked nice enough. Tami wondered if she had the nerve to start a conversation. It made her nervous just to think about it. But she forced herself.

"Hi," Tami called. "I'm Tami. You're the girl who teaches the origami class, aren't you? The girls in my cabin really like that class."

The girl stared at Tami and smiled. Then she saw another counselor coming up the path. In another second the blonde girl and her friend were happily chatting with each other as they walked back down the path.

Tami felt embarrassed. She was sorry she had opened her mouth. It seemed to happen like that so often. Whenever she tried to talk to people, it all went wrong. Somehow they didn't seem interested in knowing her.

Before Tami turned and went inside, a figure came from a row of cabins nearer the lake. It was Sommer. She had had a bad day. On the horseback ride, Dane had ignored her. At the barbecue she'd seen him sitting with Tami. She was burning with resentment.

"There you are, Tami. I suppose you think you're a big shot because you went after that kid," Sommer said bitterly. "But the truth is that nobody was impressed. Vanessa and I only let you hang out with us at school because you were so pathetic. But you have to face facts. People don't like you, and they never will!"

Fighting tears, Tami hurried into the cabin and closed the door. She knew she should ignore Sommer. She pretended she hadn't even heard her cruel words.

But each one had struck Tami like a blow. Maybe what Sommer said was true. Maybe she would never find her own nice friends. Maybe she would always be lonely. Always on the outside looking in.

♦ • ♦

At breakfast the next morning, Tami stared down at her scrambled eggs. She was determined not to embarrass herself again by approaching another stranger. But when she looked up, she saw a friendly looking girl with short curly black hair and big eyes. The girl was talking to another girl. But she looked happy and bubbly. Just like the sort of person with a big enough heart to make room for many friends, not just one or two.

Tami thought about it. Should she take one more chance? Should she risk another snub, another hurt? Could she find the courage to try one more time? She remembered what Aneal had said about bravery. Tami remembered what

Grandfather had told her. And she thought about the courage it had taken to ride the big silver horse, even though she was shaking with fear.

"Hi," she finally said. "I'm Tami."

"Hi," said the girl. "I'm Alicia. Where's your cabin?"

"I'm in Cabin 6," Tami said.

"Then we're almost neighbors! I'm right around the corner in Cabin 7. Hey, what are you and your kids doing later on? I'm an astronomy nut. I want to take the kids out to study the stars tonight. You want to bring your girls too? I think we'll have fun. I baked some moon cookies. They're just big white sugar cookies. But calling them moon cookies is more fun," Alicia said with a giggle.

"That sounds really good," Tami said excitedly. "I work in the kitchen, so I can bring lemonade for us to drink and some paper cups."

"Oh, wow! Would you?" Alicia said.

"Sure," Tami said.

Alicia grinned. "This is great! I've been here for three days now, and I haven't made any real good friends. How come you and I didn't find each other sooner?" She threw her arm around Tami's shoulders.

"I … I don't know," Tami said. She was so surprised and overcome with joy that she could barely speak.

"I'll get the moon cookies and meet you outside about nine, Tami. You bring your girls and the lemonade. I can hardly wait. This is going to be fun!" Alicia said.

◆ ◆ ◆

Hours later, the stargazing party was underway. Alicia said, "Let's get together tomorrow and make planetariums with our kids. Oh, but you probably want to go horseback riding. I heard about what you did yesterday. And I know there's another ride scheduled for tomorrow."

"Ugh, no. I'm scared of horses," Tami said quickly. "I'd love to work on a planetarium!"

"You too?" Alicia giggled. "You mean it's not just me? I've been afraid to tell a living soul how terrified I am of horses!"

The two girls threw their arms around each other, laughing. They made plans for the next day at camp. Tami was thrilled. She felt her confidence surge.

Sitting nearby, Aneal couldn't help overhearing the conversation between the two counselors. And she couldn't help but laugh along with them—even with her mouth full of moon cookies.

Comprehension Questions

Recall

1. Why did Tami take the job as a camp counselor?

2. What happened to make Vanessa and Sommer turn away from Tami?

3. What secret fear was embarrassing to Tami?

Analyzing Characters

1. Why did Tami ask to be assigned as a kitchen helper?

2. What two words could describe Sommer?
   - *spiteful*
   - *compassionate*
   - *vain*

3. What two words could describe Aneal?
   - *lonely*
   - *superstitious*
   - *insecure*

Vocabulary

1. What kind of horse would be called spirited?

2. Sommer and Vanessa tried to humiliate Tami in front of Dane. What does *humiliate* mean?

3. Aneal's parents were involved in a fight over custody of their daughter. What does *custody* mean?

Drawing Conclusions

1. When Sommer said that Dane had complained about Tami's whining, what conclusion did Tami draw?

2. What conclusion did Tami draw about how she got trapped in the barn?

3. What conclusion had Tami reached about approaching strangers?